LEADER

LOYALTY

NOX PRESS

books for that extra kick to give you more power
www.NoxPress.com

LEADER

LOYALTY

Elise Leonard

NOX PRESS
books for that extra kick to give you more power
www.NoxPress.com

Leonard, Elise
LEADER (a series) / Loyalty
ISBN: 978-1-935366-30-0

First Nox Press printing: April 2010

books for that extra kick to give you more power

**This book is dedicated to
the family members and friends of
our servicemen and servicewomen.**

To all of those who have served:
Thank you.

To all of those who have the wonderful traits
that are the titles of the books in this series:
Thank you.

The world becomes a better place
when people have these attributes.

So... no matter what the past brought,
or what the present holds,
or what the future brings...
be a LEADER!

~Elise

loy-al-ty –noun

1. the state or quality of being loyal; faithfulness to commitments or obligations.

2. faithful adherence to a sovereign, government, leader, cause, etc.

3. an example or instance of faithfulness, adherence, or the like: *a man with fierce loyalties.*

CHAPTER 1

The sun was shining.

The air was warm.

There was a sense of peace on the base.

The children were playing.

The birds were singing.

It was as if all was right in the world.

The three women hung out as usual. They were the best of friends.

Brought together by their husbands' jobs.

Had they not met their husbands? They probably would never have met.

But now they were friends.

Good friends.

The kind of friends one longs for.

They looked out for each other.

They were there for each other.

They helped one another.

They could share anything. And knew they would not be judged.

They could ask anything. And knew they would find answers.

They could say anything. And knew they would he heard.

They could do anything. And knew they would find support.

There is no other way to put it...

They had each others' backs.

CHAPTER 2

"Money's getting tight," Kim said.

"For me too," Belle said.

They looked at Maria.

"What?!" she said. "You think things are not the same for me?!"

"I can barely pay for groceries," Kim said softly.

She waved at her son Kerwin.

He was playing on the monkey bars.

"I'm behind on payments to the dentist,"

Belle said.

Again, they looked at Maria.

Maria laughed. Then she shrugged.

"We eat a lot of pasta. And live with our cavities," she said.

The women laughed.

"How are you laughing through this?" Kim asked Maria.

"Look. We're all poor. All of our husbands are away. We can either cry about it. Or we can laugh about it."

Kim smiled.

"You're right," she said to Maria.

"Okay," Maria said. "So. You, Kim, can have pasta for a few days."

Maria turned to Belle.

"But how are *you* going to pay your dentist?" Maria asked.

"I don't know," Belle said. "What would *you* do?"

"Well... if you really want to know? I

wouldn't pay him."

Belle looked shocked.

"You just wouldn't pay? *Ever*?"

Maria laughed.

"Of course I'd pay the man. But not first. First I'd buy food."

Kim nodded.

"Kids *do* need to eat," Kim said.

"Then I'd pay for heat to keep the kids warm," Maria said.

"They do need to stay warm," Kim agreed.

"Then," Maria said. "*Then* I'd pay the dentist."

Belle looked at Maria.

Maria shrugged.

"Hey. You asked me what *I* would do."

Maria waved to her daughter Autumn.

Autumn was playing with Kerwin on the monkey bars.

"That's what *I* would do," Maria said.

CHAPTER 3

Two weeks later, things were worse.

It got colder. So the heating bills got higher.

But life went on for the three women.

It was a school day. So they had to take their kids to school.

They did this every day.

They would meet outside. Then they would walk their kids to school together.

It was a nice time to catch up.

Belle and Maria waited for Kim.

"Where do you think she is?" Maria asked Belle.

Belle shrugged.

"I don't know," she said.

Maria nodded.

"It's not like Kim to be late," Maria said.

Maria called Kim on the phone.

"Is everything okay?" Maria asked Kim.

"I have to keep Kerwin home from school. He is sick today. Go on without me."

"Okay," Maria said.

"But you guys can stop by my place. After you drop off the kids," Kim said.

So they did.

CHAPTER 4

"Come on in," said Kim.

"Okay," Belle said. "I have a few minutes to spare."

Maria laughed. "Free coffee? You don't have to ask *me* twice!"

They had a routine.

When they were at Kim's house? They always sat around her table. In her kitchen.

They even sat in the same chairs. Every time they were in Kim's house.

It was like they had assigned seats.

"Want some cookies?" Kim asked.

Maria laughed.

"I've never said no to cookies!" Maria said.

Belle laughed too.

"Me neither," Belle said. "But I probably should."

Belle always complained about her looks.

She could pass for Queen Latifa's twin sister.

Maria waved off Belle's comment.

"You're gorgeous and you know it!" Maria told Belle.

Belle smiled with pleasure.

"Thanks," she said.

"And I thought you said your husband liked..." Maria looked at Belle. "How does he say it?"

Belle laughed.

"He likes women with a little meat on their bones," Belle said.

"So have a cookie or two," Maria said. "And *enjoy* them!"

"They *are* chocolate chip," Kim said.

"Your favorite, Belle," Maria added.

Kim brought over a pot of coffee.

She poured out three cups.

She knew how Belle and Maria liked their coffee.

Belle liked hers with just milk.

Maria liked milk and sugar.

"How are you doing with money?" Maria asked Belle.

Belle shook her head.

"Not well," Belle said.

"Did you call the dentist?" Kim asked.

Belle shook her head.

"No. Not yet."

Just then there was a knock at the door.

The women looked at each other.

"Were you expecting someone?" Belle asked Kim.

"No."

Maria reached into a cabinet.

She took out a heavy pan.

She handed it to Belle.

She took out another one. For herself.

"We'll stand behind the door," Belle whispered.

"Say the word *taco*, if you need us," Maria said.

Kim smiled.

"Yes, *taco* shouldn't come up in a normal conversation."

That was how they did things.

How they protected themselves and each other.

Together.

Belle and Maria moved behind the door.

They raised their pans.

Ready for action, if needed.

Kim looked at her friends. She nodded quickly.

Then she opened the door.

Three men stood outside.

They were in full dress uniform.

They took off their hats when Kim opened the door.

Kim got dizzy.

Her knees started to buckle.

She felt weak.

Her stomach rolled.

She thought she would lose her breakfast.

"Taco," she whispered as she collapsed.

CHAPTER 5

One of the men rushed to catch Kim.

He threw his hat to the ground.

Belle and Maria did not know what was going on.

The hat rolled into the house.

"Did she say taco?!" Maria shouted.

"Yes," Belle replied.

Belle smashed her pan down.

Right on top of the rolling hat.

Maria jumped from behind the door.

Her pan was ready to make contact.

The man with Kim in his arms reeled back.

He bumped into the two other men.

They lost their balance.

But not before Maria raised her pan again.

"Let her go!" Maria screamed.

The pan was arcing down.

The man's head was at the other end of the arc.

"Whoa, whoa, ladies," he said.

He shifted Kim in his arms.

He now held her with his right arm.

His left arm shot up.

Bonk!

It took the impact of the pan.

The other two men just stood there.

"Would you *please* take those pans from these ladies," he said.

The men took the pans from Belle and

Maria.

But not before Maria got another swipe at the man holding Kim.

Bonk!

This time it hit him on the head.

The two men not holding Kim laughed.

"We should send these two into battle," the second guy said.

"Forget the M16. We can arm them with cooking pans!"

Kim's eyes started blinking.

She looked up at the man who was holding her.

"What's going on?" she asked.

"Beats me," he said.

"You opened the door," the second man told Kim.

"Then offered us a taco," the third man said.

"Then you fainted," the second man said.

"Then these two came flying out from

behind the door."

The two men in the back laughed.

"You got ambushcd, sir," the second man said.

The man stood. He scooped up Kim.

He made a face.

"Thanks for your help," he told the two other men.

He walked into Kim's kitchen.

Then he placed her in a chair.

"I think you ladies should all sit down," he said gently.

Kim looked at Belle and Maria.

"I knew it was bad," she whispered.

The women reached their hands out.

They clasped each other's hands.

They sat there. Holding hands.

Waiting to hear what the man said.

But at the same time...

Not wanting to hear what he had to say.

CHAPTER 6

The head guy looked at Maria.

"We went to your house first."

Then he looked at Belle.

"Then we went to your house."

He looked at Kim.

"We were told to try here."

"But you were also on our list," the second man said.

The head guy shot him a look.

A dirty look.

All three women saw it.

They squeezed their hands tighter.

The head guy cleared his throat.

"We would like to speak with each of you," he said gently.

The women didn't move.

"Alone," he added.

The women looked at each other.

"Whatever you have to say to me," Maria said. "You can say in front of them."

"It's the same for me," Belle said.

"Me too," Kim said.

The women were clutching each other's hands.

They were holding on as tightly as they could.

It was as though they were trying to hold each other up.

Physically.

Supporting each other.

Through their hands.

The head man did not look happy about this.

His face was sour.

The women knew what he was about to say.

It had to be bad news.

And they did not want to make it easy on him.

Why should they?

CHAPTER 7

"Are you sure?" he asked the women.

"Yes," they all said.

He nodded.

Then he cleared his throat again.

He turned to Kim.

"Your husband is coming home in two weeks," he said.

Kim cried out.

This was not what she'd thought he would say.

"You mean he's not dead?" she asked.

He shook his head.

"No ma'am."

Kim started to cry.

They were tears of joy.

Not tears of sadness.

Maria and Belle squeezed her hands.

She smiled from beneath her tears.

"He's coming home," she whispered.

Maria and Belle smiled at Kim.

They were happy for her.

Then the man turned to Belle.

"Your husband is coming home in two weeks, too."

Belle also let out a soft cry.

She closed her eyes and smiled.

"He's coming home," she whispered.

Maria and Kim squeezed Belle's hands.

They were happy for their friend.

Very happy.

Things were hard for Belle lately.

So the women were glad that Belle's husband was coming home to help her.

Then the man turned to Maria.

Maria was always trying to see the bright side of things.

Always the one to make the women laugh.

"Two weeks for me too?" she asked.

Maria's head was cocked.

Her face was shining with joy.

Her dimples were showing.

They always showed when she was very happy.

"No," the man said. "Your husband is coming home tomorrow."

Maria's hands flew to her face.

"Tomorrow?!" she said.

She looked at her friends.

"I have to clean the house," she said.

"He won't care," Belle said.

"He cares more about *you*. And Autumn,"

Kim said.

"You're right! I have to buy a nice dress," Maria said.

The women giggled.

"And do my hair!" Maria said.

Her hands ran through her hair.

"It's such a mess!" Maria said.

"Wow. Your husband's coming home tomorrow," Kim said.

"You're so lucky!" Belle said.

Maria laughed with joy.

"I have so much to do!" she said.

"I'll get Autumn from school," Belle said.

"Don't worry," Kim said. "We'll take care of Autumn."

"You go do what you have to do," Belle said.

"You guys are the *best*!" Maria said.

Then she popped out of her seat.

"Please don't mind my leaving," Maria

said.

And then she flew out of Kim's house.

*   *   *

No one had noticed the small boy watching from the living room.

No one had noticed Kerwin.

With all of the excitement? They'd forgotten that he was sick that day, and home from school.

CHAPTER 8

Maria had flown out of there.

She'd left so quickly. The man could not stop her.

"I have to speak with her," the man said.

Belle and Kim looked at each other.

"I'm sure she's sorry she hit you with the pan," Kim said.

"She was just trying to protect Kim," Belle said.

"Please don't get her into trouble," Kim

said to the man.

"No," he said. "It's not that."

He looked at the other two men.

"This did not go as planned," he said.

"She's sorry she hit you," Kim repeated.

"No, it's..." the man started to say.

He stopped talking.

It seemed as if he didn't know what to say.

"Do you know where I can find her?" he asked Belle and Kim.

They shook their heads.

"No," Belle said.

"Knowing Maria?" Kim said. "She could be anywhere."

"I really need to talk with her," the man said.

"Just tell us," Belle said.

"Yes. We'll tell her," Kim added.

He shook his head.

"I can't," he said.

He got up to leave.

He handed each woman a business card.

"If you should need me for anything. Please call me."

Belle and Kim looked at each other.

They were both thinking the same thing.

Their husbands were coming home in two weeks.

Their lives will now go back to normal.

Why would they need anything from *him*?!

"And please give this to your friend," he said.

He put a third business card on the table.

"Please have her call me the moment you see her," he added.

The women left the card on the table.

"Please," he repeated. "The moment you see her."

* * *

Maria never did call him.

CHAPTER 9

TWO WEEKS AFTER THAT DAY IN KIM'S KITCHEN WHEN MARIA HIT THAT MAN WITH A PAN...

"Have you heard from Maria?" Belle asked Kim.

"No. Have you?"

Belle shook her head. "No."

"I hope she's okay," Kim said.

"She said she'd call when she got

settled."

Kim looked at Belle.

"I guess she's not settled," Kim said.

Belle nodded.

"So, how's J.D. doing?" Kim asked.

Belle's face showed sorrow.

"He's in such agony, Kim."

Kim reached out and took Belle's hand.

"It's awful," Belle added.

Kim nodded.

"I don't know how he can stand it!" Belle said softly.

Kim patted Belle's hand.

"I mean, the pain," Belle added quickly.

Kim smiled sadly.

"I knew what you meant."

A tear rolled down Belle's cheek.

"And he says such awful things," Belle whispered.

"Like what?"

"Like how he looks like a monster. And

how I should leave him."

"What do you say back?" Kim asked.

"That he's being silly."

Belle started to cry.

"But he just goes on and on about it," she wailed.

Kim looked afraid to ask.

"How *does* he look?" she asked softly.

Belle closed her eyes and cried.

She couldn't even answer.

Kim hugged her friend.

Things had changed so much. In such a small amount of time.

Life was now so different.

And would not go back to the way it once was.

Ever.

"This is not what I had planned," Kim said.

"It's not what I had planned, either," Belle said.

The two women kept on hugging.

It was as if they were clinging to a life raft.

"He says his mom named him well," Belle said.

Kim looked confused.

"J.D.?"

Belle nodded. "Yes."

"I don't get it," Kim said.

"He says that J.D. now stands for Just Done."

Kim raised her eyebrows.

"I still don't get it," Kim said.

"He says, 'Stick a fork in me. I'm Just Done.'"

Kim gasped.

"That's horrible!"

"I know," Belle said.

She wiped at a tear.

"It hurts my heart when he says it," she added.

CHAPTER 10

The women hugged tightly.

"This is so hard," Belle said.

"I know," Kim said.

Belle stepped back.

"Oh my goodness," she said. "I've been so selfish!"

She looked at Kim.

"I didn't even ask," Belle said.

She looked closely at her friend.

"How's Cesar?"

Kim took a deep breath.

Then she let it out slowly.

"It's hard to say," Kim said.

Belle looked at Kim.

"He's got a nick-name for himself, too," Kim said.

Belle raised an eyebrow.

Kim rolled her eyes and shook her head.

"He calls himself... Hop-Along."

"That seems in poor taste," Belle said.

Then Belle snorted a laugh.

"But it's right up there with J.D.'s 'Just Done,'" Belle said.

"This nick-name thing? It must be a guy thing," Kim said.

"It must be," Belle agreed.

"But he's not fooling me," Kim said.

"Fooling you? About what?"

"He's trying to pretend he's okay."

"Maybe that's what he needs."

"He just lost his *leg*, Belle!"

"I know."

"And you know how active he's always been!"

"I know," Belle said again.

"For goodness sake! He's a runner! He runs *marathons*."

"I know," Belle said.

"He puts on this good face," Kim said.

Then she looked angry.

"He even jokes about it!" Kim shouted.

"Isn't that better than telling you to leave him?" Belle asked.

Kim shook her head.

"No. I don't think so," Kim said.

"What do you want him to do?"

"I wish he would be honest with me," Kim said.

Kim looked at Belle.

Kim's eyes were so troubled.

Belle hugged her friend.

"I wish he would be honest with me. But

to even *think* that, makes me really afraid," Kim said.

"Why?"

Kim looked at Belle.

"You know what they say," Kim said.

Belle shook her head.

"No. What do they say?" she asked Kim.

Kim smiled sadly.

"They say, *Be careful what you wish for.*"

For some reason? That made both women cry.

They cried together.

They knew that they could be honest with each other.

They knew that they could speak their minds. And no one would think lesser of them.

CHAPTER 11

"I know how you feel, Kim," Belle said.

"This is so hard," Kim wailed softly.

"I know."

"It's hard for J.D. and Cesar," Kim said.

"I know."

"It's hard for the kids," Kim said.

"I know. They are confused."

Kim took out a tissue.

She dabbed at her eyes.

"They are not used to seeing their fathers

like this," Kim said.

Belle nodded.

"And we are not used to seeing our husbands like this, either," Belle said.

Belle must have thought of J.D. at that moment.

She shivered with her thought.

"Is he that bad, Belle?"

"It looks as if most of his face has been melted off. His ear is gone. And so is his eye. Most of his hair and scalp have been burned off."

"I'm so sorry," Kim said. "For him. For you. For the kids."

"He's *so* angry," Belle whispered.

"He has a right to be," Kim said softly.

She gave Belle some tissues.

"Don't you think so?" Kim asked.

Belle took a deep breath.

She let it out slowly.

"Yes. He has a right to be angry. But..."

Belle stopped talking.

She looked ashamed.

"What?" Kim asked.

Belle shook her head.

"No. I shouldn't say it."

"Go ahead," Kim told Belle.

She took her friend's hand.

"You can say whatever you want to say," Kim told Belle.

"I know that," Belle said.

"I won't judge you," Kim said. "I promise."

"I know that," Belle said.

"So go ahead, Belle. Get it out. Say what you want to say."

"But I feel guilty."

"This is *me* you are talking to," Kim said. "You can say anything."

Belle nodded slowly.

"His anger? It is more than I can handle right now. I just can't handle it all."

CHAPTER 12

"That's why I'm afraid to wish for Cesar to be honest with me. I'm afraid I won't be able to handle it either," Kim said.

"So why are you wishing for it?" Belle asked.

"Because I feel he needs to get it out."

"Maybe he can't right now," Belle said.

"It's not good to bottle things up."

Kim looked at Belle.

"They'll explode," Kim explained.

Belle thought about that.

"This just happened to them, Kim."

Belle tilted her head as she thought.

"Maybe, like me, Cesar needs time to take it all in."

It was Kim's turn to think.

"Yes," Kim said. "Maybe."

Belle laughed.

"You *always* say that Cesar takes a long time to think things through."

"That's true," Kim said.

"Like picking out your couch," Belle said.

Kim started to laugh.

Belle joined her.

The two women laughed their heads off.

"It took him *three weeks* to pick a couch!" Kim said.

Her body shook with laughter.

"And I only gave him two to choose from!"

"And, if I recall. Wasn't one so hideous that he'd be *forced* to pick the other one?"

Kim bent over with laughter.

"Yes! I showed him the one I *wanted*. And the ugliest couch in the entire store!"

Tears were rolling down Kim's eyes.

"No. I'm wrong. It was the ugliest couch in the whole *world*!" Kim said.

Belle was laughing, too.

"It really *was* ugly!" Belle said.

"And he *still* couldn't decide quickly!"

Belle tapped Kim's hand.

"Remember when your car died?" Belle asked.

"And he had to pick out a new car!" Kim said loudly.

Bouts of laughter shook the women.

"It took him so long? The *new models* came out!" Kim recalled.

"Maria had to drive you and Kerwin everywhere," Belle said.

"I thought Maria was going to kill my husband!" Kim said.

Kim was shaking with laughter.

"Maria *screamed* at Cesar," Belle said.

Then the two women spoke at the same time.

"*Cesar, would you please PICK SOMETHING?! Here. Take MY car!*"

Bell and Kim kept laughing.

"Maria *would* have given you guys her car, too!" Belle said.

"Cesar knew that," Kim said. "That's why he *finally* made a choice."

Their laughter died down.

They looked at each other.

"I miss Maria," Belle said.

"I do too," Kim said.

"I hope she's okay," Belle said.

"Me too," Kim said.

CHAPTER 13

**FIVE YEARS AFTER THAT DAY IN
KIM'S KITCHEN WHEN MARIA HIT
THAT MAN WITH A PAN...**

"How's J.D. doing?" Maria asked.

"He just had more skin grafts," Belle said.

"And is he still so angry?" Maria asked.

"Not so much anymore."

"That's great," Maria said.

They both sounded relieved.

J.D.'s anger was hard on Belle.

And Maria was glad that her friend's life was getting a bit easier.

Maria was glad for J.D. too.

"I'm glad he let it go," Maria said.

"Yes," Belle said. "Me too."

"It's hard to live with that much anger," Maria said.

Belle did not reply.

"And I know it's hard for the family too," Maria said.

"Probably harder," Belle admitted. "Because we feel so helpless."

Maria hugged Belle.

"Hey," Kim said. "I want in on that hug. Sorry I'm late."

The three women hugged.

"How's Cesar doing?" Maria asked.

"Great. He's got a new leg. It doesn't hurt him so much."

CHAPTER 14

TEN YEARS AFTER THAT DAY IN KIM'S KITCHEN WHEN MARIA HIT THAT MAN WITH A PAN...

The women hugged.

"You look so great!" Maria said to Belle.

"So do you!" Belle replied.

"I can't believe Kerwin is graduating from high school!" Maria said to Kim.

"I can't believe he's going to college!"

Kim said.

"How are you doing with that?" Maria asked.

"I'm sad and I'm proud," Kim said. "Both, at the same time!"

"I'll be going through that next year," Maria said. "With Autumn."

Kim hugged her friend.

"You won't go through it alone," Kim said. "Belle and I will be there for you."

Maria looked sad for a moment.

"Thanks," she said.

But then she cheered up.

"Life is always better with friends."

"And speaking of friends," Belle said. "Which one of you is going to tell my husband how bad his wig looks?"

"He still thinks he needs a wig?" Kim asked.

"His exact words? '*It makes me look less freakish.*'"

"Does it?" Maria asked.

"Yes, as long as it's not this last wig he picked out."

Just as Belle said that, J.D. walked into the house.

The minute Maria saw him? She burst out laughing.

"My gosh, J.D.!" Maria said. "What *were* you thinking about?!"

He grinned crookedly.

"Not a good look for me?" he asked.

"It's not a good look for Bo Derek. For *you*? It's worse!"

"But my afro is too big. They don't wear them that big anymore," J.D. said.

"I love the big 'fro!" Maria said. "Give it to *me*."

"Well, if I'm not going to wear the afro or the corn-rows? What am I going to wear?!"

"Buy a smaller 'fro, bro!" Maria said.

J.D.'s smile was wide.

"Great idea, Maria! Thanks."

J.D. looked at his wife.

"Now why didn't *I* think of that?!" he asked Belle.

"Most likely because that wig of blond corn-rows is too tight!"

Maria grinned.

"It *really* looks bad, J.D.!" Maria said.

J.D. looked from Maria to Belle to Kim.

All three women were nodding.

"It has *got* to go!" Belle said.

J.D. looked at Maria.

"You want it?" he asked.

He peeled it off his big, bald, scarred head.

Maria laughed.

"No," she said. "That thing is hideous! But I *do* want the big 'fro."

J.D. gave her the big afro wig.

CHAPTER 15

**TWENTY-FIVE YEARS AFTER THAT
DAY IN KIM'S KITCHEN WHEN
MARIA HIT THAT MAN WITH A PAN...**

"I cannot *believe* Kerwin bought you a house!" Maria said.

Kim scoffed.

"Yeah. My son can buy me a *whole* house. But can my husband buy me a new couch? No."

"I can't make up my mind!" Cesar said.

"I only gave you *two* to choose from!" Kim said to Cesar.

The women giggled.

"The same types of choices?" Belle asked Kim.

The three women left the room to talk.

"How ugly is the second couch *this* time?" Maria asked.

"Remember the last one?" Kim asked.

"The red and green one with Santa faces all over it?" Belle asked.

"Who could *forget* that?!" Maria said.

"My husband was *thinking* about that couch last time," Kim said. "As one of our choices!"

Maria made a face.

"I couldn't sit on Santa," Maria said.

"And not in June!" Belle added.

"He was really thinking about it?" Maria asked.

"Maybe he just didn't want to spend the money," Belle offered.

"Yes," Maria said. "Maybe *that's* it. Because no one has taste *that* bad!"

"It's not about taste. It's about making a decision," Kim said. "And by the way? *This* second couch choice is even *uglier*!"

Kim's doorbell rang.

J.D. was there to pick up Belle.

The women could hear the guys talking.

They'd been friends as long as the women had been friends.

"Hey," Belle said. "Let's let J.D. help Cesar pick the couch."

Maria laughed.

"You're talking about the large black man who once wore blond corn-rows?"

The three women cracked up.

J.D. came to the doorway.

"What are you three up to?" he asked.

His latest wig was a jheri curl.

Maria stared at J.D. "Is that real hair?"

J.D. smiled. "Yes, in fact. It is."

"Can I touch it?" Maria asked.

J.D. grinned.

"You'll have to ask my wife."

Maria looked at Belle.

Belle laughed.

"Feel away," she said. "I did the same thing when he came home with it."

"Get the pictures of the couches," Maria whispered as she walked past Kim.

Kim ran out.

Then she ran back in with the pictures.

"What's going on in there?" Cesar called from the living room.

Maria grabbed the pictures.

She showed them to J.D.

"Which one do you like?" she asked.

He pointed to the ugly couch. "That thing's *ugly*!"

"Go tell that to your friend!" Kim said.

CHAPTER 16

FIFTY YEARS AFTER THAT DAY IN KIM'S KITCHEN WHEN MARIA HIT THAT MAN WITH A PAN...

Maria hugged Kim and Cesar.

"You look more beautiful with every passing year, Maria," Cesar said.

Maria waved him off.

"Pfft. That's just the Latino male in you talking, Cesar," Maria said. "That, or you forgot to bring your glasses again."

Kim and Cesar laughed.

So did their son Kerwin.

"Thank you for driving your folks here, Kerwin," Maria said.

"You're welcome, Mrs..."

Before Kerwin could finish, Maria spoke.

"Kerwin. You're not eight anymore. You're fifty-eight. Almost sixty! For goodness sake, you *can* call me Maria!"

Kerwin smiled.

"You're welcome... Maria," he said.

Maria smiled.

"I'll come back in two hours to get you," Kerwin told Kim and Cesar.

As he left, Belle and J.D. appeared at the door.

"Come in. Come in. Please," Maria called to them.

Maria hugged J.D. and Belle.

"You're looking as beautiful as ever,"

J.D. said to Maria.

"Pfft. That's just the dog in you talking, J.D.," Maria said. "That, or I've gained even *more* weight. We all know how you like a woman with some meat on her bones!"

"You got *that* right," J.D. said.

Then he thwacked Belle's very round backside.

Belle giggled.

"I'd tell you two to get a room," Maria said. "But I want to visit with you first."

They all sat in Maria's small living room.

"Please," Maria said. "Make yourselves at home."

She went to the kitchen and came out with a tray.

Yes. They had made themselves at home.

Cesar's leg was off.

It was leaning against the couch.

J.D.'s wig was off.

And hanging over the lampshade.

J.D.'s scars still covered most of his face and head. But the wigs still made him feel better when he was out in public.

Maria pointed to the lamp.

"I see you got a new wig," Maria said.

"I went for a gray one this time," J.D. said.

Over the last fifty years? J.D. had gone through quite the variety of wigs.

Maria's favorite was still the huge black afro.

"You still have the big 'fro?" J.D. asked Maria.

"Sure do," she said. "I put it on when I have a bad hair day."

"I'll give this one to you when I get a new style," he told Maria.

"Thanks," Maria said with a laugh.

"I hear the ladies like a gray-haired man," J.D. said.

"*This* one does," Belle said.

J.D. and Belle smiled warmly at each other.

"Just don't go to corn-rows again," Maria said.

"Why not?" J.D. teased.

He knew the answer.

"It wasn't a good look for you."

"But you liked the fade, right?" J.D. asked Maria.

"Yes," Maria said. "That looked good."

"You think they make dreadlocks in gray?" J.D. teased Maria.

"I'm sure they'll make *anything* if someone will buy it," Maria said.

J.D., Belle, Kim and Cesar laughed.

They spent their time talking. And laughing.

Mostly about the old days.

CHAPTER 17

There was a knock on the door.

"I wonder who that could be," Maria said.

"You're not expecting anyone?" Belle asked.

Maria shook her head. "No."

"Should I go in the kitchen?" Belle asked.

"Why?" J.D. said. "Is your husband coming, and you need to hide?"

Belle looked at her husband.

"Yes, J.D., we need to hide from my jealous husband."

Kim, Cesar, J.D. and Maria all laughed.

"No. I meant, to get a *pan*," Belle said. "I was thinking of that man. That day. Fifty years ago."

"The one Maria conked with a skillet?" J.D. asked.

The men had heard the story.

Many times.

They were even proud of their wives. Thought it was a good way to protect themselves.

"It was a *pan*, J.D.," Maria said. "Not a skillet."

J.D. laughed.

"Beg my pardon," he said.

The knock got louder.

A woman called through the door.

"Mom? Are you home?"

Maria's face lit up.

"It's your daughter," Cesar said. "Autumn."

Maria looked at Cesar.

"You spend too much time with senile people, Cesar. I *know* my own daughter!"

Maria rushed to the door.

Well, as fast as a seventy-something woman could rush.

Maria swung open the door.

"Well, if it isn't my lovely daughter and great granddaughter," Maria said loudly.

She closed the door a little bit.

Kim and Belle knew why.

"Quick, Cesar, put your leg on!" Kim whispered.

"And J.D., you need to put on your *hair*," Belle said in a stage whisper.

Cesar grabbed his leg.

J.D. got his hair.

"We don't want to scare the child!"

CHAPTER 18

The cutest little girl ran into the room.

"I'm not scared of *you*," she told J.D.

"But I'm scared of you," J.D. said to the child.

She kissed his scarred cheek.

Then she skipped over to Cesar.

"I'm not scared of you, either!" she said.

She hopped onto Cesar's lap.

"You promise?" Cesar asked the child.

"Knock on wood," the girl said.

Then she reached down to thump Cesar's fake leg.

It was clear that this was a routine done many times before.

Autumn turned to close the door.

But Kerwin was standing there.

"I'm back, guys. Ready to go?" he asked Kim and Cesar.

"Has it been two hours already?" Kim asked her son.

"Yup. Ready to go?"

Kim looked at Maria.

"Our time together always goes by so fast," Kim said.

Belle and Kim and Maria hugged.

Then J.D. joined them.

"Group hug!" he said.

They all turned to Cesar.

"Come on, dear," Kim said.

All five hugged together.

"Same time next year? At our house?"

Kim asked.

Belle and Maria nodded.

"God willing," Maria said.

J.D. shook his head.

"I don't know if I want to go. Did you buy a new couch yet?" he asked Cesar.

"No," Cesar said. "I can't find a good one."

Kim huffed.

"He means he can't make up his mind!" she said.

Then the oldest five people in the room laughed again.

The little girl turned to Autumn.

"Grandma? I don't get it. What's so funny?"

Autumn grinned.

"It's a secret," Autumn told the little girl. "Between the five of them."

And then Kim, Cesar, J.D. and Belle left Maria's house.

CHAPTER 19

"Great grandma?" the girl asked.

Maria smiled.

"Yes, Lily?"

"Grandma says that you've been alone a long time."

"Yes, that's true."

"Don't you get lonely?" Lily asked.

"No," Maria replied. "I have memories of your great grandfather. They are with me. Always."

"Great grandpa was in the war. Wasn't he?"

"Yes he was."

Maria stood up.

"It's time for milk and cookies. Would you like some?" she asked Lily.

Lily got excited.

"Yeah! Sure! I've never said no to cookies!"

Autumn looked at Maria.

"Now where did she learn *that* line?!"

Maria grinned.

"Beats me," Maria said. "But *I've* never said no to cookies *either*."

There was a twinkle in Maria's eye.

It flashed right before she went into the kitchen.

Lily turned to Autumn.

"Grandma?"

"Yes?"

"When did great grandpa come home

from the war?"

Autumn's mind went back to when she was about Lily's age.

It was a long time ago.

Fifty years.

She was at school.

When the bell rang, Belle had come to get her.

"Your father is coming home tomorrow!" Belle had said.

Autumn was so excited.

She'd missed her father so much!

And now she'd finally get to see him.

He'd been away so long.

"Where's Mommy?" Autumn had asked Belle.

"Buying a new dress. And getting her hair done."

Autumn was so excited.

It was very hard to sleep that night.

Her mother, Maria, was singing and

dancing around the house. And Autumn didn't want to get into trouble for being up so late.

So she flashed her flashlight at Kerwin's window.

She hoped he was still up too.

Kerwin was a year older. So he stayed up a little later.

So he was up.

Two minutes later she heard the tap on the glass.

Autumn opened up the window.

"Can't sleep?" Kerwin asked.

"Yeah," Autumn told him. "I'm too excited."

"I heard it all today. While I was home. You know. Sick. These three men came and said our dads are coming home. I have to wait two weeks. But you're lucky. You're dad's coming home tomorrow."

Autumn couldn't imagine being happier.

She was lucky! Her dad was coming home tomorrow. Poor Kerwin had to wait two more weeks.

It took forever for the morning to come.

But now? Now that Autumn knew what that next day would bring?

She wished she had never woken up.

Yes. Her father *had* come home from the war the next day.

But he had come home in a casket.

The door of the kitchen swooshed open.

Maria came in with cookies and milk.

Autumn looked at her mother.

She really was an incredible woman.

Without ever saying a word? Maria had taught them *all* a lesson...

Love lives on. And loyalty lasts forever.

We hope you liked this book in the

LEADER

series.

We hope you will read
all the books in the series:

HONOR

COURAGE

RESPECT

SERVICE

INTEGRITY

COMMITMENT

LOYALTY

DUTY

Want comedies?

Try reading...

THE SMITH BROTHERS

We also have...

the very funny

A LEEG
OF HIS OWN

series.

Everyone has it
within them
to be a

LEADER

Do you?